Leila's Cl

By

Rafael Eesa

Copyright © 2024 Rafael Eesa

ISBN: 978-1-917601-12-2

All rights reserved, including the right to reproduce this book, or portions thereof in any form. No part of this text may be reproduced, transmitted, downloaded, decompiled, reverse engineered, or stored, in any form or introduced into any information storage and retrieval system, in any form or by any means, whether electronic or mechanical without the express written permission of the author.

Chapter 1

"How are you beautiful?" The red rabbit whispered gently to a turquoise dragon, which was just as big as an average sized house.

A faint and gentle blink of one of the turquoise dragon's eyes had glanced the red rabbit's head.

"Leave me alone!" The dragon groaned in an almost excessively dismissive tone.

"Hmmm...." The red rabbit hummed to himself and then shouted, "Fluffy ball, argh!"

The red rabbit turned into a ball and rolled in a silly manner along the dragon's neck, up down, up down the rabbit eagerly played, which was surprisingly very smooth. The turquoise dragon, who by the way had amazingly metallic smooth reptile like skin. A dragon who was almost not entirely dragon, burst out laughing with a gentle and kind tone to her voice.

"I knew you were not mean and nasty, see!" The red rabbit exclaimed with such happiness in his voice.

After two seconds of laughing, the metallic dragon had stopped, there was a still almost spiritual silence.
"By the way, I am not beautiful", the turquoise dragon reluctantly said. "I used to be quite pretty, but not anymore." The dragon said and immediately sighed having said that.

"You are beautiful, you are just not like you were before you had touched the platinum fountain." The red rabbit answered with assertive conviction.

"How is it that you know about the platinum fountain?" The turquoise dragon surprisingly asked.

She was quite puzzled about the fact a mere rabbit had known about the platinum fountain. To the turquoise dragon, whose elegance and way of conducting herself even when speaking was that of a queen's. She saw the red rabbit as an immature and very confused individual, whose main aim was to annoy others, however deep down in her big heart, which was almost pulsating out of her chest, she knew he was quite unique.

"The same thing happened to me when I touched the platinum fountain", the red rabbit answered with a big smile on his face.

"That means that it turns whoever touches it into an animal!" The turquoise dragon shouted, but it was a good type of shouting, the type a person does when they are happy and excited.

Chapter 2

The cave in which the metallic turquoise dragon had lived in was dark but had a few strawberry scented candles. Strawberries reminded her of her hometown, in which they would grow and sell many strawberries. It was her only source of comfort. That is until the red rabbit had told her that he had touched the platinum fountain. The rabbit was extremely furry with floppy ears.

"My name is Leila", the turquoise dragon cheerfully said.

"My name is Knight", the red rabbit said with a gentle smile with a bush of fluff surrounding his mouth. "I have a map in my possession that may help me and you to return to our normal states", knight said graciously.

Knight was the type of person, who would behave very childlike at first with an individual. He would feel more comfortable starting conversations this way and would afterwards not feel shy to show his gracious and gentle nature.

Knight used his back left foot, furry as it was, there were tiny claw like nails at the ends of his feet, to cut the string that lay around his chest and back. He used the string to keep the map on his back. Leila was quiet, eagerly awaiting to see if the red rabbit had anything useful in his possession. Poor Knight was struggling, but eventually he cut the string loose.

"Finally!", Knight exclaimed with such a happy sigh of relief.

"Okay, this is it!", knight said almost to remind Leila that he had something useful in his possession.

He carefully laid the map out on the floor of the cave. Leila carefully studied the map, glancing at every minute detail she could see on the map.

"This map is interesting, but how do you know if it has anything to do with helping us to change back?" Leila asked Knight.

"That is because the paper of the map is stained with solidified liquid platinum!" Knight answered in a calm and gracious way.

"I see, this is quite unique!" Leila said in a very excited manner.

Finally, Leila had found a somewhat vague lead on how to potentially return back to the way she once was before. It had been five hundred years since she was, hence, why she was sad and reluctant to engage in a conversation with anyone let alone a medium sized red furry rabbit with floppy ears.

The beautiful Leila was so special, and the poor person had not even realised it, even when she was a woman. Even as a woman, her life was quite sad, with people staring at her with always a confused look on their faces. No one ever talked to her. She would practise talking to the portraits, which were laid across her village. Leila had spent five hundred years straight thinking about why this was the case, as a result, her poor head had become quite tired and would normally keep her head laying on top of her arms as she lay down in her cave.

The map had a tree in the middle surrounded by daisy flowers. The map was twenty centimetres by thirty centimetres. Leila stared at the platinum stained map with a very obvious smile on her face. For the first time in five hundred years, Leila was smiling, enthusiastic and happy.

"I recognise that tree!" Leila suddenly said.

"Really, I have been looking for that type of tree for forty years straight!" Knight said in state of shock.

Knight had scoured the land for forty years without even finding a tree that had even a slight resemblance to the tree on the map. Both Leila and Knight were so happy and relieved that at long last they had found some sort of lead on how they may find a way to return as people.

The tree on the map appeared very twirly at the top of the tree, and had numerous almost leglike roots, but it was obvious to tell that it was a tree and not indeed a person. It had star shaped leaves with multicoloured gemstones on the leaves. No one could really tell what type of gemstones they actually were. For all anyone knew, they could have been multicoloured diamonds, or different types of gemstones that have different colours; such as amethyst, garnet, citrine, topaz or emerald. One thing was for certain though, and that was, the tree on the map was no ordinary tree. The map also had thorns drawn on the edging of the map. It looked almost like a decorative border; however, it did have a meaning, but what could it be?

"That tree is roughly twenty miles from here, but it is hidden within a forest via secret passage", Leila eloquently explained.

"May I ask, how you know the exact whereabouts of the tree?" Knight curiously enquired.

There was one problem with Knight's overall behaviour, although he was gracious, he was also quite nosy. Leila turned her head, so that she was exactly facing Knight. She wanted to make sure that he was going to fully understand what she was about to say.

"Once I had been turned into a dragon, I was travelling to find a suitable cave for myself to live in, I had come across that tree. My tail had touched a twig near a bush on the floor and I fell into a tunnel. Once I had come out that tree on the map was there." Leila elegantly explained to the attentive Knight.

"Alright! That sounds good to me, let's go!", Knight excitedly exclaimed with a huge smile on his face, to the point almost all of his teeth were showing, which by the way were quite small.

Leila was excited, but she started wondering what hint or potential secret that unusual tree may hold. She was remembering when she had seen the tree five hundred years ago, that was when she was starting to get used to being a dragon. At the time she had never touched the tree, due to the fact she was worried she may have broken the tree. She was worried, because of the fact she was a dragon and quite a big one at that. Leila was always courteous towards nature, as was Knight.

"Wait!" Leila suddenly said.

"What's the matter?", Knight said with a slightly concerned look on his face.

"I must first have my breakfast." Leila said in a fairly annoyed tone in her voice.

"So, what would you like?", Knight asked considerately.

"I have some strawberries at the back of the cave that I would like. I will go get them now, and then we can go." Leila said with a gentle smile on her face.

"Would you like some?", she asked.

"Yes, please!", the cheerful red rabbit answered, with such happiness in his eyes.

Knight was the type of person that was rarely, if ever offered anything by anyone. The fact that Leila had offered him some juicy strawberries made him so happy. Knight knew the fact that the strawberries were juicy, because he knew that Leila was the type of person that would only eat the best quality produce that lay out there, or in this case lay in the cave.

Knight had been a red rabbit for two thousand years, but he did not wish to disclose this to Leila yet, because he was worried, she may laugh at him or ridicule him. Before, Knight was an average adult, but he would help people in the city he once lived in. Unfortunately, people saw him as the cause of the problems. He would work at an anvil, making horseshoes and little metal nails. He would work long hours, however, despite that he would still have the time to help people. He once helped someone find their lost horse. Poor Knight wanted someone to kindly offer him something, the way Leila did for such a long time.

"Here they are. Take as many as you like." Leila said with a gentle sweet smile on her face.

"Thank you!", Knight joyfully said.

The strawberries were quite big, they were the size of an average sized tennis ball. There was in total twenty strawberries that lay on the floor, with some green leaves underneath them. Leila didn't like plates, so she would use leaves and other natural resources as a plate; such as straw and, believe it or not moss from inside the cave. To Leila, the cave was her home, she had become so accustomed to living there and just occasionally popped out her cave to find some suitable fruit and vegetables to eat. She would not venture very far. She would only go at most around a hundred metres around her cave.

Leila and Knight started eating the strawberries in a calm and relaxed manner. Leila and Knight started staring at each other in a gentle way. After fifteen minutes, they had finished eating all of the strawberries. There was then a slightly awkward silence.

"That was actually very tasty, thank you." Knight said with a full belly, he was slightly struggling to speak due to the fact he had eaten eight big strawberries.

"You're welcome." Leila said ever so gently.

She was surprised Knight had eaten eight full strawberries, but was ever so happy that he had accepted her gift, and also enjoyed the berries.

"I think we both need a little time to digest the strawberries." Leila pointed out.

She knew the red rabbit was in no condition to do any major travelling yet, how ever eager he may have been.

"You're right", Knight groaned whilst he tried to lie on his side to make his stomach feel a bit better.

"So how long have you been a rabbit?", Leila enquired.

"Oh, I don't really remember to be honest. I am quite forgetful you see. Sorry about that." Knight said in a very sad tone.

Knight was hoping that Leila would believe what he just said. Leila looked at Knight's eyes, which were a vivid purple almost glowing colour. Leila's eyes were a gentle blue colour, with very long eyelashes that were jet black.

"I know you're lying to me." Leila said in a way that she almost knew that Knight was going to lie to her the moment she asked him that particular question. "You can tell me the truth Knight, I will not laugh at you. I understand that certain circumstances are not as easy to resolve as others may think. I promise I won't poke fun at you." she beautifully said with a slightly sad and concerned look on her face.

"Okay, the truth is that I have been a red rabbit for two thousand years. I have become quite used to the fact that I am a rabbit and don't take it personally, you know." Knight explained while smiling in a gentle way.

He felt quite bad for making Leila a bit sad. Both Leila and Knight were concerned for each other, and wanted to help each other sincerely.

"I'm sorry to hear that." Leila said with a lot of sadness in her voice.

"Don't you worry, beautiful!", Knight said assertively and added, "Luckily we have a lead on how we can both return as people."

Chapter 3

After twenty minutes of both the orange dragon and the red rabbit digesting their strawberries, they eventually left the cave. The sun was beginning to set.

"I know a shortcut", Leila pointed out.

"Okay", Knight acknowledged.

Leila lowered her head and said, "Climb onto my back, that way I can fly both of us there!"

"Oh yeah, that would be quicker, than both of us walking there on foot, because my feet are quite small." Knight stated with a small giggle in his voice.

Knight rolled into a ball, like he did in the cave, and rolled on her head and towards her back, and opened up.

"I am officially ready!", Knight affirmed with excitement in his voice.

"Hold tight!", Leila added. She started to flap her wings slowly, and gradually faster.

Leila's wings were quite beautiful, they were metallic orange, like her body, but had pink pearls on her wings. There were around thirty pink pearls on each of her wings. The pearls had a very gentle pink hue, which was a tiny bit metallic when the sun shone on them. The beautiful pearls were about the same size as an average sized cabbage.

"What amazingly coloured pearls!", Knight sincerely said.

"Thank you, but it's nothing special", Leila persistently said.

"Oh, I beg to differ!", Knight happily said. Contrary to what Leila said, she had pearls on her wings, due to the fact she was extremely kind and gentle. Leila took off with Knight, and headed in the direction of the mysterious tree.

The environment of which they were in currently, was extremely quiet. When Leila was flying, trees were rustling from the wind, as a result of her pretty wings flapping fairly vigorously. She flew with elegance and tranquillity. Elegance was one of Leila's main traits, even before she was a dragon. She would do even everyday tasks with natural elegance, and enjoyed doing even hard tasks; such as picking strawberries from quite tall trees with a large ladder, and carving wooden ornaments.

Knight's fluffy fur was moving, due to the amount of wind blowing against him. Leila was flying very fast, she had already covered two miles in just five seconds.

"This breeze is just so relaxing", Knight joyfully said.

"Sorry to cut your relaxing time short, but we're here", Leila calmly said. She suddenly stopped and Knight fell off. "Oh dear, I'm so sorry", she said with sympathy in her voice.

"Oh, don't worry, I'm fine", Knight said with a gentle smile.

Knight knew that she didn't do it on purpose. It had been five hundred years, since she had last flown. It was only at the beginning of when she had become a dragon. Since she was so sad all those years, she never had a drive to fly at all.

Poor Leila was getting used to the fact she was so fast when she was flying.

"This is the forest where the secret passage is", Leila explained gently.

"Okay, so lead the way", Knight said quietly, he had become slightly tired and drowsy. This was because, he was not used to travelling at such high speeds. Leila could quite easily see that Knight wasn't feeling one hundred percent, thus she took her initiative, and decided to pick him up, and hold him gently in one of her hands.

"There, there, you will be okay", Leila sweetly said to Knight. She started walking slowly, to make sure that Knight wasn't disturbed too much. "Oh, there's the twig", she said with a happy and sigh of relief.

She was inside, quite worried that it would not be there, and may have moved after all those years. She used her tail to gently touch the twig, which lay in exactly the same place as it had five hundred years ago. The secret passage opened, and Leila fell into the tunnel, while still holding Knight. They were both travelling in the tunnel for ten seconds, until they both came out of a metal pipe.

"This is absolutely amazing!", Knight exclaimed.

He started feeling better all of a sudden upon looking at the mysterious tree.

"Yes, it is quite magnificent", Leila agreed.

She started studying the tree, by looking at every detail of the tree in a scrutinous manner.

The tree was much bigger than what Knight had been expecting. The unique tree was roughly one hundred and twenty metres in height, with a width of around thirty metres. The tree had various carvings on it, mainly featuring twirly lines, and a bit of stars that were also carved. Sparkling daisy flowers surrounded the tree, which were one and a half metres tall.

"These flowers are so pretty", Leila said with admiration in her voice.

"Yes, these are called daisy flowers. They are quite pretty, I must say", Knight graciously said to Leila with a little smile on his furry face.

"I've never seen such beautiful flowers in all my life!", Leila reaffirmed.

The daisy flowers were not there the previous time Leila had come to see the mysterious tree.

"Wait a second, if you were here before, how come you never saw these flowers before?", Knight asked in a confused tone.

Poor Knight was overwhelmed with all this information, and was quite tired, hence why he was a bit confused.

"They were not here the last time I was here", Leila pointed out.
"Oh, I see", Knight said in a calm manner.

Suddenly, a door opened, which was on the tree, but there was no visible evidence that there was a door prior to it being opened. The door was part of the actual tree, and was creaking loudly, upon it being opened.

"Why hello there!", a woman gently said.

"With all due respect, who are you?", Knight curiously asked the lady.

"My name is Hilda, and I am the gatekeeper of this tree, and it's surroundings", Hilda gently explained.

"My name is Leila, and this is Knight", Leila said.

Knight was excited, because he was almost one hundred percent certain that Hilda would know something useful, in how both him and Leila could go back to the way they were as people.

Hilda was covered head to toe in silver-coloured bandages, which were fairly shimmery. Her eyes were only visible and her mouth. Hilda's eyes were an amethyst green colour, and were big and round. Her lips were cherry blossom pink colour with a gentle almost glow like effect.

"Why don't you both come inside?", Hilda enquired.

"I don't think I will fit in that small door", Leila reluctantly said.

"That's not a problem, I will just open the bigger door", Hilda softly said.

She went inside the tree briefly, and opened the larger door from inside. The small door was part of the larger door. Now that the big door was open, Leila and Knight made their way inside of the mysterious tree.

"By the way, would you like some lime juice?", Hilda asked.

"Yes, please!", both Leila and Knight said.

Hilda gave both Leila and Knight cylindrical copper cups, and got a jug of lime juice. The jug of lime juice was made from glass that was lime green and poured juice for both of them. She then poured some for herself as well. The inside of the tree was very cosy, with vine leaves decorating the interior of the tree, as well as glowing multi coloured gemstones on the walls. Leila sat on a velvet dark green cushion, which was quite large. Whilst Knight was sitting on a blue velvet armchair. Hilda was sitting on a purple velvet sofa, gently sipping her lime juice.

"So, what brings both of you here?", Hilda gently asked.
"We both touched the platinum fountain and wish to return as people", Knight eagerly explained.

Leila had already finished her lime juice, due to her cup being relatively small to her.

"Okay, what you will need to do is, you will need to make your way to the city of ruby", Hilda explained.

"What lies in that city that may help us?", Leila enquired.

"Well, there is a blue flower hidden inside the city. I do not know where though, but once you obtain it, a passage to the town in the clouds will open for you. After that, you will have to figure it out for yourself, I'm afraid. I don't know anymore than that, sorry." Hilda explained while looking at Leila.

Hilda knew that Leila was growing to be quite impatient with the fact that she was still a dragon, and had still certain tasks to fulfil, until she could return to her true state.

"Don't worry Leila, this predicament you and Knight are in is not as difficult to undo as you think", Hilda strongly affirmed.

"Okay, so where is the city of ruby?", Leila asked while studying the interior of the tree.

Knight was enjoying drinking the lime juice and was attentively listening to both what Leila and Hilda were saying.

"The city of ruby is located two hundred miles east of where the amethyst tower is", Hilda explained and gently had a sip of her lime juice.

"But where is the amethyst tower?", Leila gently asked.

"I don't actually know where it is located, unfortunately, sorry", Hilda said in a sad tone.

Hilda wanted to help both Leila and Knight, but she wasn't aware of certain locations of certain landmarks. She was only aware of names of places, along with vague directions, but no specific landmarks to aid them in their journey. The town in the clouds was quite well known to the people in which Leila use to live with in her hometown. The city of ruby was not actually two hundred miles east of the amethyst tower, it was three hundred miles west of the amethyst tower. Hilda was unfortunately not very good with directions, and was very forgetful, but had the purest of intentions. The amethyst tower was similar looking in structure to a lighthouse, but it was to do with being a pivot point to different elements with different lands. The amethyst tower was at the centre of different elements, depending on the direction a person would venture to; for example, north is snow, south is hot and dry, east is windy, and west is mild weather.

Currently, Leila and Knight were just below the amethyst tower. The tree in which they were in, was just below the purple tower.

"You know, I think I might know where the amethyst tower is", Knight joyfully said with a small grin on his face.

"Where?", both Leila and Hilda asked curiously.

"Above the ground pf where the tree is that we are in now", Knight graciously said.

The mysterious tree, which they were in, had a flat like ceiling, and was a hint that the mysterious tree was slightly below ground level.

"Oh, I just realised, that is true, what Knight just said. I was also appointed five thousand years ago, to being the caretaker of the amethyst tower!" Hilda affirmed with a gentle smile and happy sparkle in both of her eyes. "By the way, let me check the records in the tower up in the tower, just to make sure that the city of ruby is two hundred miles east of the amethyst tower", she stated.

"That sounds good to me!", Knight cheerfully affirmed.

"Do you have maps up in the tower?", Leila asked.

"Yes, I do, I just remembered I have quite detailed records, which are old maps, but at least they are accurate." Hilda said with a playful tone in her voice.

Leila, Knight and Hilda were all feeling optimistic and content. Leila and Knight had a quite solid lead on how they could return to their true states, and Hilda remembered her other duty, which she had forgotten about for a considerable amount of time.

Chapter 4

"So, has everyone finished their lime juice?", Hilda happily enquired.

"Yes, it was very enjoyable, thank you", Leila answered.

"Yes, thank you", Knight said.

"Okay, follow me. There should be a very long staircase here in this tree, that leads up to the amethyst tower", Hilda explained.

Both Leila and Knight followed where Hilda was walking, and they were led to a large, wide stone staircase. The staircase was an indigo colour, with bits of stone chipped away from the steps.

"Did you make this staircase?", Leila eloquently asked.

"Oh no, my mother was the one who made this staircase. She was very practical and resourceful. Unfortunately, she left, and I do not know where she is, but hopefully I will see her again soon." Hilda said while attempting to still have a faint gentle smile on her face.

Hilda, Leila and Knight were walking up the stone staircase.

Leila then asked; "What is your mother's name? If it's not too personal of a question."

Leila was eager to ask, due to the fact that hopefully her and Knight may encounter her, or can ask if anyone has seen her recently, while they are travelling.

"My mother's name is Jessica. She almost always wears a metallic indigo coloured suit of armour. Mother was quite fond of that colour. She wears armour as a way of increasing her stamina and endurance, although, I don't think I would like to try it", Hilda gently explained.

"Oh, I see, me and Knight will keep a look out for her while we are travelling", Leila said in a concerned manner.
"Okay, we have reached the end", Hilda stated.

There lay a giant amethyst door with no handle. The door was like a faceted amethyst gemstone in the shape of a heptagon and was only able to be opened by Hilda's hand moving in a certain way, upon touching the right side of the heptagon door. She had opened the door, and Leila and Knight followed through. The amethyst tower seemed quite desolate, with a spiral staircase, that was in the clockwise direction and a little bookshelf on the ground floor. The bookshelf was made of solid silver in it's purest form. The composition of the silver was had no added minerals to it, as a result, it was as shiny as a polished mirror. Hilda preferred that the silver bookshelf was not an alloy, because she liked to touch the softness of the metal in it's natural state. "This is quite interesting", Knight joyfully said with an enthusiastic tone in his voice. "It is quite lovely", Leila said while looking around the interior of the amethyst tower.

"I believe the maps are on the top shelf", Hilda said quietly.

She walked towards the silver bookshelf, and began reading the spines of the books, which had old maps of the whole landscape.

"I think this is the one", Hilda said while trying to concentrate on what content was inside each book of maps.

She looked inside a book, which was a square shape, and had a cover and back made of tree bark. She was skim reading the book in a very quick manner.

"Oh, well it's a good thing I checked the map. It seems that the city of ruby is actually three hundred miles west of this tower." Hilda said and gave a huge sigh of relief. "That it better, that the city of ruby is on the west side of the amethyst tower, and not on the east side of the tower." She said with a lot of happiness.

"Why's that?", Leila quietly enquired.

"That is because, the east side is very windy, but the west side has gentle mild weather. Your journey should be more pleasant", Hilda stated and gave a big smile.

"I wish you both the best, and if you ever have any questions, I will be here in the amethyst tower, or under where the mysterious tree is." Hilda explained in a joyful manner.

"Thank you for everything", Leila gently affirmed.

"Yes, thank you very much", Knight said whilst smiling.

"I'll open the west door, but remember that the city of ruby is only three hundred miles west of this tower, it's not that far in theory, just a reminder." Hilda mentioned.

"Okay, we will bear that in mind, thank you", Leila assertively said.

Hilda opened the door, and both Leila and Knight walked out of the amethyst tower.

"She was right, the weather here is gentle and mild", Knight stated.

"You can climb on my head", Leila said.

"Oh, you mean we are going to fly there?", Knight asked.

"Yes, otherwise it would take us very long", Leila explained.

She gently lay her head down on the ground, Knight then climbed on to her head. Once Knight was on her head, she flapped her wings and began flying in the direction of the west. Leila started thinking about when the time would come for her to be able to turn back as a person, what she would actually want to do. She wasn't really too sure with where she would like to live in, and how possibly she could make some friends to speak to.

"Don't worry, everything will be fine", Knight comfortingly said to Leila.

Knight could sense that Leila was thinking about her problems, he therefore wanted to comfort her, so that she wouldn't worry at all. Both Knight and Leila were kind and caring individuals, as a result, they would comfort each other.
"Okay, I won't worry, and thank you Knight, that's very thoughtful of you", Leila replied.

"Is it okay if we have a little break?", Leila asked.

"Yes, we can find some fruit if you would like", Knight graciously answered.

Leila gradually stopped flapping her beautiful wings and slowly landed. She was more cautious than the last time, as a result Knight did not luckily fall off like the last time Leila had stopped flying suddenly. Knight jumped off, once Leila had landed on the ground.

"We covered thirty miles at least", Leila elegantly said.

"You can fly very fast, so we could reach the city of ruby quite quickly, even if we have a little break for now." Knight enthusiastically said.

In the meantime, while Leila and Knight were relaxing, Jessica was roughly four thousand miles north of the amethyst tower. She was looking for her pickaxe, which she seemed to have misplaced. She was wearing her metallic indigo suit of armour and looking through the snow. At last, she found it, she swung her pickaxe with such force, it split the rock she was aiming for in two. A necklace fell out of the rock, that was made of gold. The gold colour was very rich, the chain was a simple weave of three golden wires intertwined, and the pendant was a coin with a smooth polished texture.

"Hmmm.... I can give this beautiful necklace to my lovely daughter Hilda", Jessica said.

Jessica would often say things that she was thinking, in order to help her remember things.

She was mining eagerly, because she was looking for a very rare hot pink coloured gemstone with a unique hue. She wanted to obtain it, so that she could give it to her daughter Hilda. Jessica's daughter would look through books and see pictures of the gemstone, and it would cheer Hilda up. Jessica decided to leave Hilda without prior notice to mine for that gemstone, and to only come back once she had obtained it. When Jessica appointed her daughter Hilda, as the gatekeeper of the mysterious tree, and the amethyst tower, Hilda became quite upset. She also felt that she was carrying more responsibility than what she was able to carry. Jessica was eager to cheer her daughter up, and felt quite bad for giving her those responsibilities.

Jessica had been away from her daughter for seventy years. She felt that she was getting close to finding the hot pink gemstone and was almost certain it was somewhere in the northern part of the land. The reason she thought that, was because a lot of gemstones that she had already mined were very colourful. Unfortunately, though, she had no purple or pink shaded gemstones, however that did not deter her from mining in the north for the beautiful jewel.

"I think I will try that rock", Jessica softly said.

Meanwhile, Leila and Knight were looking at the nearby trees to see if any of them had any fruit.

"No, this one doesn't have any fruit", Knight said with a hint of slight annoyance in his voice.

"This one has some", Leila happily said.

The fruit on the tree was similar looking to an apple, but was deep purple in colour. Leila picked six fruits from the tree and gave Knight three out of the six.

"No, it's fine, I want only two fruits. I had more than I needed the last time I ate some fruit. I need to know my boundaries, you know", Knight explained.

"Okay, if that's how you feel", Leila acknowledged.

They both began eating.

"This quite nice. It's sour, but in a pleasant and mild way", Leila gently stated.

"I agree with you on that", Knight happily said.
The landscape, which they were in was quite cosy. There were big trees, that had bushy, almost fluffy like leaves. The grass was gentle and felt almost like silk. The sun had just gone down and it was night. The sky was glowing with a purplish hue. There lay bright stars in the sky of many different sizes flashing on and off. The moon was big, it covered about one tenth of the sky in the direction of the sky, in which the moon was. The moon was a beautiful turquoise colour, that had a hint of metallic shimmer around it.

Chapter 5

"Sorry to bring this up now, but is it okay if we sleep here for a bit? I feel quite tired", Knight said quite slowly.

"Yes, that's fine, we have done a lot today anyway", Leila elegantly said.

Leila and Knight leaned against a giant tree, and decided to rest for a little while. They both fell asleep relatively quickly, they were both exhausted. They were both sleeping for six hours, then they woke up.

"That was a nice nap", Knight said quietly.

"Yes, it was a nice nap", Leila said with a hint of happiness in her tone of voice.

Leila and Knight both felt recharged and refreshed after their nap. It was still night time, but they were both eager in making their way to the city of ruby. Leila started pondering as to whether the whole city was made entirely of ruby, or if the "ruby" aspect of the city was just a metaphor, or just a name given to the city, because there may be an abundance of ruby.

"What are you thinking about?", Knight enquired curiously.

"I was just wondering if the city of ruby is completely made of ruby, or if it's just a metaphor", Leila softly answered.

Knight began to think for ten seconds.

"I don't think the whole city is made of ruby, because that would have required so much effort to build. It's probably just a metaphor, like the buildings may be painted a ruby red colour", Knight answered.

"Oh, I see that seems more plausible", Leila said. "I am a bit worried about the fact that once we reach the city of ruby, I will not really be allowed in." She reluctantly said in a sad tone.

"Why's that?", Knight asked.

"I don't think in cities, they have dragons the size of houses walking around casually, not to mention the fact I may break some buildings by accident. I wouldn't like to break anything, you know", Leila explained.

"I see your problem. Ah I just remembered reading in a book once many years ago, that there is this gemstone that is able to shrink a person. Unfortunately, it's only temporary, it only lasts for four hours", Knight eloquently explained.

"How would we obtain it?", Leila gently asked.

"I just remembered something, I was wondering why that name Jessica rings a bell. I read in a book a while ago, that she is the gatekeeper of certain types of rare gemstones. That means we have to find Hilda's mother Jessica, before we can go to the city of ruby." Knight said with a lot of enthusiasm.

"Where do we start to even attempt to look for Jessica?", Leila enquired.

"Well, first we need to find a region where the gemstones that are mined, are very rare. She may be looking for some new rare gemstones", Knight explained.

"That's a good idea", Leila happily stated.

Both Knight and Leila got along well together. They also deeply cared for each other. They both felt and knew that they cared for one another, but it was a feeling they were not familiar to.

They both looked at each other and said, "I care about you, you know."

They said this to reaffirm the deep caring bond they had for one another.

Jessica felt as if someone, or in this case two people needed her help, and immediately began running. She was so fast that if someone was watching her running, they wouldn't really be able to see her. Naturally, she ran in the direction of where Leila and Knight were. Ten minutes had passed until she had arrived in front of Leila and Knight.

"Oh, you're Jessica", Knight said with fascination in his voice.

"Yes, I am Jessica", she said confidently.

"I am Leila,,, and this is Knight", Leila said.

"I sensed you needed my help, so I came running . What is it that you need?", Jessica enquired.

"We need a special gem that will shrink Leila, at least for a few hours. I read in a book many years ago that such a gemstone exists", Knight explained.

"I see, because I assume you wish to enter a city or town", Jessica said.

"Yes, we both wish to enter the city of ruby, but I'm worried that I would break some buildings by accident, because I am quite big." Leila elegantly articulated.

"Yes, I understand", Jessica stated in a tone in which she almost knew what Leila was about to say.

Jessica put her hand in her pocket and brought out a green coloured gemstone, which was about the same size as an average sized raspberry. Jessica had pockets on the sides of her beautiful suit of armour, that merged with the armour she wore.

"Which one of you would like to hang on to this gemstone?", Jessica kindly asked.
"I can, because I have something similar to pockets on my sides near my legs!", Knight said with enthusiasm.

"Leila may lose it, because she doesn't really have pockets like me, no offence", Knight added.

"You know I am aware of the real reason you want to hang on to it, right? You have a passion for gemstones and like touching them." Leila beautifully said with a big smile on her face.

"How did you know that?", Knight asked with a surprised tone in his voice.

"The way your eyes lit up when you saw the gemstone", Leila replied.

Jessica gave Knight the gemstone and said, "Please make sure you look after this gemstone, as it is very rare."

"Yes, I shall look after it, I promise!", Knight said firmly.

"I have a question, how do I use the gem to shrink, when I need to?", Leila gently asked.

"You just hold the gemstone, and you must have the intention to shrink, and you will shrink, however the effects only last four hours. Then you will be your normal size again", Jessica articulated.
"Okay, thank you", Leila said.

"Thank you", Knight joyfully said.

"Oh!, I just remembered, your daughter Hilda asked us if we saw you to tell you that she would like you to come back to her, because she misses you and she's quite sad. She's upset about the fact you've been away for a while", Leila explained.

"I had no idea that she was sad, because I thought she knew that I was going to be away from her temporarily. Hilda, my beautiful daughter saw years ago in a book, this certain hot pink gemstone and liked it a lot, so I wanted to mine it and give it to her as a gift. I am a gatekeeper of certain types of rare gems, but the one she saw in the book, unfortunately I do not have." Jessica explained in detail.

"Is it a hot pink stone with a very vivid colour?", Knight enquired.

"Yes, that's the gemstone", Jessica replied.

"The reason I am asking, is because years ago, I overheard two people talking about a gemstone which fits that description. They said it's located in some vast forest, underneath a giant boulder", Knight explained.

"I see, I know where that is, Knight thank you very much!", Jessica said with happiness.

Knight, Leila and Jessica were all looking up at the sky and admiring how beautiful it was.

"The moon is bigger and brighter than usual, it makes me quite happy just to look at." Jessica calmly stated.

"The sun will come up within two hours from now", Jessica added.

"I hope you find the gemstone you are looking, for your daughter", Leila said with a gentle smile.

"Hopefully, I will", Jessica said.

Knight was leaning against one of Leila's feet, Knight was relieved to have the gemstone that would shrink Leila, but he was also tired, he didn't want Leila to know that. He wanted to reach the city of ruby as quickly as possible. He wasn't rushing to get there, but he didn't want to take long either. Knight loved Leila, which gave him his drive to embark on this expedition with a lot of enthusiasm. If he was by himself, he wouldn't have much enthusiasm, and would be extremely sad. Leila also loved Knight but was shy and did not know how to say it.

"Well, I will be on my way, thank you for everything, both of you." Jessica said with happiness.

"You're welcome, and thank you for your help", both Leila and Knight said at the same time.

They then both looked at each other, and they each gave a gentle smile. Jessica darted off and was gone.

"Well, luckily that solves the problem you were having", Knight said.

"Yes, I'm glad that I can now shrink", Leila stated.

"Did you know that the gem can also enlarge someone, like me, so I would be a similar size to you." Knight enthusiastically pointed out.

Both Leila and Knight stared at each other.

"Just joking!", Knight said whilst laughing out loud with a big smile on his face.

"I already knew you were joking Knight, I know how you are very well, you know." Leila softly stated.

"Okay, if you say so", Knight quietly said.

Knight and Leila, both knew each other well, although they didn't know each other prior to them meeting recently.

"We can watch the sun rise together soon", Knight suggested.

"Yes, it would be nice to watch the sun rise with someone, instead of watching it alone", Leila said sadly with a gentle smile on her face.

"I will always be here to help you when you need me, and to cheer you up." Knight said in a cheerful manner.

Leila and Knight both leaned up against a giant tree, which had berries sprouting from it. They patiently waited. Two hours had passed, and the sun began to rise, all of the colours of the landscape were now clearly visible. The sun was a gentle orange colour, similar to that of a citrine gemstone.

"It's beautiful!", Leila said with such fascination in her voice.

It was actually the very first time, kind Leila had ever seen the sun rise.

"This is your first time seeing the sun rise, isn't it?", Knight enquired.

"Yes, but how did you know?", Leila asked with a bit of confusion as to how Knight had known that.

"It was the way you spoke, it was in such fascination, as if you had never seen it before. See I know you very well also." Knight graciously said.

"Okay, whatever makes you happy", Leila said with a gentle smile.

After thirty minutes of both the orange dragon and the red rabbit watching the sun rise, they decided to travel, and make their way to the city of ruby.

"We have roughly about two hundred and seventy miles left to cover, until we reach the city", Knight pointed out.

"Luckily, I fly roughly two miles in five seconds, so we should reach the city quite quickly", Leila said.

Knight climbed on to Leila and sat on her neck. After that, Leila took flight, and she started flying faster than she than she had done previously without realising it.

"Whoa! This is quite fast, I like it!", Knight shouted.

Within a few minutes, they could see buildings, which were made of genuine ruby. Each building was unique; some were quite tall and thin, and some were quite wide and average in height, for example a typical house but slightly wider.

Leila slowed down and quickly stopped completely.

Knight got off Leila and said, "I had no idea the city of ruby's buildings were actually made completely of ruby!"

"It's so pretty", Leila softly said.

Both Leila and Knight were staring at the buildings in fascination.

"Okay, it's time now for you to shrink", Knight abruptly said.

He took the green unique gem out of his side pocket near his legs.

"Okay, I'm ready", Leila said with a slight hint of hesitance in her voice.

"Don't worry, it's harmless", Knight gently said.

"I'm just worried I will become too small", Leila said with concern.

"You'll probably just shrink to a similar size to me", Knight said cheerfully.

Leila took the gemstone from Knight's paw and shrunk herself. She had instantly shrunk and was roughly the same size as Knight.

"See! I told you that you would shrink to a similar size to me!", Knight joyfully said.

"Well, I'm glad that I am not too small", Leila happily said.

"Now we go to find the blue flower, so we can go to the town in the clouds. I don't know what to do after that, though", Knight said in a quiet tone.

"We will figure it out once we are there", Leila softly stated.

Both of them then entered the city filled with ruby buildings.

Chapter 6

Leila and Knight strolled into the city. There were many people walking on the streets of the city. The floor was made of a light-coloured marble, which had a gentle yellow tint. There were stalls, which were quite wide, some of them covered one fifth of the whole street.

"This city is quite impressive", Knight said.

"I agree, but it is quite big, a bit too big for my liking", Leila stated.
"I think it's quite nice. Anyway, I think we should ask that man over there for directions as to where the mysterious blue flower may be", Knight suggested.

"Okay", Leila agreed.

"Excuse me, do you know where that mysterious blue flower is?", Knight asked the man at the stall.

"I am not too sure to be honest, you can try ask the lady at the flower stall over there", the man replied.

"Okay, thank you", Knight said.

The stall Knight had asked at with the man was selling clothes, which were quite colourful, and weaved in a very unique way. Leila was staring at the clothes, she had never seen clothes which were that colourful.

"We can buy some, once you have returned to normal", Knight quietly said.

He felt sorry for Leila, she saw some nice clothes that she liked, but was not able to wear them.

"Don't worry about it, I'm fine", Leila said gently.

They both walked to the flower stall. It had all sorts of different varieties of flowers, which bared different colours and shapes. A woman with light blue coloured hair was the person operating the flower stall. The stall was compact and was made of orange wood. The lady was wearing purple loose robes, which had silver-coloured patterns on the sleeves of the robes.

"Excuse me, but do you know where we can find the mysterious blue flower?", Knight asked the lady at the flower stall.

"How cute! I have never seen a talking rabbit before. You are quite fluffy. The mysterious blue flower, hmm. Did you know there are many of those mysterious flowers, not just one?", the lady said enthusiastically.

"No, I thought there was only one of them", Knight said with shock.

"Yeah, well you know they are usually grown in batches of twenty once a year. However, unfortunately I have sold all twenty of mine yesterday. If you had come in the morning of yesterday, there would have been plenty, sorry." The lady explained in detail.

"No! What are we going to do now? We really needed one of those blue flowers. We can't wait until next year!" Knight said with a bit of frustration in his voice.

"Don't worry, we can maybe find another route to go to the town in the clouds", Leila calmly said with a hint of disappointment in her voice.

"Am I correct in saying that you wish to go to the town that lies in the clouds?", the lady enquired.

"Yes, we do", Knight replied.

"My name is Violet, and yours?", Violet said with a kind smile.

"I am Knight, I like your name Violet, it sounds very gentle", Knight said.

"My name is Leila, nice to meet you", Leila said while giving a faint smile.

"There is another way that you can enter the town in the clouds. The queen of his city knows how to enter the elusive town. If you would like, I can take you to the queen", Violet said.

"Yes, okay, but what about your stall?", Knight asked with concern.

"Don't worry, my sister can just watch my stall. That's her across the road", Violet answered.

Violet called her sister over and explained to her that she may be gone for a few hours or so.

"Okay, let's make our way there", Violet happily said with a big smile on her face.

The queen lived in a castle, that was completely carved out of ruby, and had four towers on the side of the castle, which spiralled upwards.

"It's not very far, probably only ten minutes away", Violet said.

"I can't wait to see the castle, usually queens live in castles, right?" Knight asked Violet.

"Yes, queens live in castles or palaces, the queen of this city lives in a beautiful castle", Violet explained.

Leila, Knight and Violet were walking past different types of stalls, some had different fruit, some had different types of tools, while others had jewellery of all kinds.

"Is this your first time seeing the city of ruby?", Violet enquired.

"Yes, it is, it's quite beautiful", Leila replied.

"Yeah, this is my first time as well", Knight stated, while looking at one of the stalls in the distance.

"I moved to this city around twenty years ago with my sister", Violet elegantly stated.

"Why did you move here? If you don't mind me asking", Knight nosily asked.

"I wanted to live in a place which has a lot of trade, because I enjoy trading and selling flowers. In other words, business is better here than where I lived before", Violet briefly explained.

The three of them were all silent for a little while. They were all thinking about what the queen might say to them upon their arrival. After all, they were going to visit the queen unannounced. They were also wondering if the queen was even in the castle. Maybe she was seeing one of her relatives. The three of them were all just hoping that everything would go smoothly.

Six minutes later, and the castle was within close range.

"Okay, here we go, I will speak on your behalf. If you want me to add anything, you let me know", Violet explained to both Leila and Knight.

"Yes, that is fine with me. Do me and Leila go inside the castle, with you?", Knight gently enquired.
"Yes, of course!", Violet said in a cheerful manner.

"I'm okay with that as well", Leila said serenely.

A royal guard was standing outside the entrance with a spear and a shield. He was also wearing armour, which was a gentle pink colour, and was metallic. The shield was also the same colour as the armour. The shape of the shield was square and had a silver-coloured trim around it. The spear had a very thin handle. Two horizontal blades sprouted at the very top of the spear. Violet, Knight and Leila approached the royal guard.

"What is your business here?", the royal guard enquired.

"We wish to see the queen about quite an important matter, if we may", Violet eloquently said.

"I'm sorry, you are not allowed to see her majesty unless you have arranged to see her in advance", the royal guard firmly stated.

"Okay, would it then be possible if we saw one of her ministers instead?", Violet said with persistence.

"No, I am sorry, but you cannot even see a minister if you have not arranged a meeting in advance", the royal guard reiterated.

Violet was thinking what to say next, when all of a sudden, a lady appeared from the castle.

"Violet, is that you? What business do you have here at the queen's castle?", the lady gently asked Violet with a slightly concerned look on her face.

The lady was worried that Violet was in need of some help, and as a result was concerned for her.

"It's not to do with me, it's to do with these two whom I have here with me. They were trying to obtain the mysterious blue flower, but I had already completely sold all of mine. They wish to go to the town located in the clouds, and since the queen knows how to access there without a mysterious blue flower, we were wondering if it would be possible for us to see her about this. However, the royal guard here says, if we haven't arranged to see her in advance, we cannot do so." Violet explained in detail.

The lady who Violet was speaking to was one of the queen's ministers. She was the minister of architecture and was extremely successful at it. Her and Violet were close friends, but they would spend time together when they were not working.

"Excuse me, royal guard, these three will come with me. I authorise it, so you will let them pass", the minister said in a strong tone.

"As you wish, you may pass", the royal guard said slowly.

"My name is Claire, and what are yours?", Claire asked Leila and Knight.

"My name is Leila, and this here is Knight", Leila answered happily.

Claire led all of them inside the castle. "Is this a castle or a palace?", Knight curiously enquired.

"It's either one, the queen refers to it as both, so it's really up to you which you prefer to say", Claire replied.

The interior of the palace was decorated with pearls on the floor along with nuggets of highly polished amethyst.

"This palace is well decorated", Leila said with a surprised look on her face.

"Yes, it is", Claire affirmed.

"I thought a castle and palace were different", Violet said.

"In a sense they are, but they're quite similar. Some kings and queens prefer to call their domain a palace, and some prefer to call it a castle. Luckily, the queen of the city of ruby doesn't really mind which of the two her domain is referred as." Claire explained in a placid manner.

There were paintings of different types of trees, some were quite geometric, and some were quite curly.

Claire didn't bother to enquire as to why both Leila and Knight wished to go to the town in the clouds. She was the type of person who would just mind her own business, and do tasks she was given in a productive manner. Royal guards were also standing within the castle.

"I will speak to the queen now, if it's okay with you three, I would like you to just wait here", Claire stated.

Four minutes had passed, and the queen along with Claire had come out.

"I am sorry, but I do not let just anyone go to the town in the clouds just like that you know, it requires effort and energy on my part. I am not willing to do that for mere passers-by. You do not even live in this city. I don't gain anything by letting you both go to the town in the clouds", the queen said in an annoyed tone.

"Well, maybe we can help with something, like working in the garden of the palace", Knight persistently suggested.

"No, I don't need work being done in my garden, thank you", the queen replied concisely.

Knight and Leila started thinking about how they could persuade the queen to help them access the elusive town in the clouds. No ideas were coming to both of them.

Chapter 7

Meanwhile, Jessica was in the vast forest Knight spoke of and was right next to the giant boulder as described. Jessica swung her pickaxe with such force, the boulder completely smashed. She eagerly started to dig where the boulder was. After seven minutes, she saw a vivid pink glow. She wasn't aware that the gemstone she was looking for was capable of glowing. She dug more, and finally unearthed the gem. What was quite strange, was that it was as if the gemstone had already been cut and polished.

"Maybe that's just the way that gemstone is", Jessica said. She was smiling and let out a sigh of relief. "Finally, after seventy years of being away from my daughter, I can at last go to her with the gemstone she wanted in my possession," Jessica stated with happiness.

She was finally relieved of worrying that she may not be able to find the hot pink coloured gemstone for her daughter Hilda. Just before she met Leila and Knight, she was starting to lose hope, but luckily had found it. Jessica then headed in the direction of the amethyst tower, so she could see her daughter after all those years.

The queen of the city of ruby had dark blue straight hair, which reached her waist. She was wearing bright pink-coloured robes, that had patches of dark red over the sleeves. She wore square gold earrings, which were dangling, and had a single ruby gemstone faceted on each earring. The queen was very firm with her decision making, but it was possible to change her mind if Leila or Knight had a useful idea that would benefit the queen.

"If you would like, we can get you some nice gemstones from the town in the clouds, if you allow us to go there", Knight suggested.

"No, I do not need any additional gemstones to what I already have now", the queen sternly answered.

Leila realised the queen wasn't easy to convince, or rather it wasn't easy to change her mind. She then had an idea, she would just explain to the queen why her and Knight wanted to go there in the first place. Leila thought that maybe the queen might feel sorry for her and Knight, and just them gain entry to the town in the clouds.

"Erm, queen, the reason myself and Knight wish to go to the town in the clouds is because we would like to return to normal, as people. We were told by a woman by the name of Hilda, to go to that town. We became animals, because we touched the platinum fountain", Leila elegantly explained in a slightly upset tone of voice.

Leila was becoming slightly concerned, whether or not, herself and Knight would be able to go to the elusive town.

"Did you say the platinum fountain?", the queen said in a surprised manner.

"Yes, that is what I said", Leila replied.

"I have been looking for it for quite some time, do you know where it is?", the queen enquired.

"The problem is, when I touched it, it vanished. Unfortunately, I do not know where it is currently", Leila explained.

"Every time someone touches the platinum fountain, it moves to a completely different location, I read it in a book many years ago", Knight explained.

"That's a shame, because I wanted to see it with my very own eyes", the queen said with a slight hint of disappointment in her voice.

The queen was thinking that if Leila or Knight knew the current location of the platinum fountain, she would be willing to let them go to the town in the clouds. Sadly, they were not aware of where it was.

"I tell you what I can do for you two, you can help me locate where the platinum fountain is currently, and when you do notify me. I will see it, and then I will open the passage to the town in the clouds. What do you say?", the queen asked.

"Very well, we will try to locate the platinum fountain", Knight said in a slightly annoyed tone, which was very faint.

The queen began to smile and started walking towards Violet. The queen explained something to Violet. The red-haired queen was familiar with Violet by mention of name from Claire, and as a result wished for Violet to accompany Leila and Knight in helping them find the platinum fountain.

"Okay, so where do we start looking for the fountain?", Knight asked with confusion in his voice.

"I know where we can start, the outskirts of this city", Violet explained in a gentle manner.

Violet guided Leila and Knight out of the castle and came along with as the queen requested.

Chapter 8

The queen began thinking about her brother, who was the one who made the platinum fountain, hence why the queen was so interested in seeing it with her very eyes. Her brother left the city of ruby at a very young age, he returned once he was an adult, but that was just to visit. He left a note just before he left; it read:

"If you wish to know why I left the city of ruby permanently, you should solve the riddle of the platinum fountain, which I made."

The queen did not disclose to Leila or Knight the reason as to why she wanted to see the fountain in person, because she felt that it was none of their business. The queen sighed and sat on a red metallic armchair and started thinking about why the fountain would move it's location entirely. Claire went outside the castle to notify Violet, Leila and Knight about something.

"There is an easy way to tell if the platinum fountain is nearby. If the ground; for example, soil, is a bit metallic grey in colour, it means the fountain is in fairly close range." Claire explained while smiling gently.

"Understood, let's get looking", Knight said enthusiastically.

"I don't feel we will be looking for it for a long time", Violet said in a calm way. After speaking briefly with Violet, Claire headed back to the palace.

Ten minutes later, Violet, Leila and Knight were at the outskirts of the city.

"So, where do we look from here?", Knight enquired with confusion.

Knight was enthusiastic most of the time, but he would fairly often be confused and puzzled.

"We will start off by taking Claire's advice, we shall look at the ground, to check if there is any metallic grey colour", Violet stated.

The three of them began to study the ground, but no one found any even vague greyness on the ground, nor any metallic tint either.

"Let's have a break for a little while. After all, things are moving fast for the both of you", Violet said gently.

Knight leaned up against a tree, which had berries on it.

"Oh, they look tasty", Leila said while pointing up at the berries, that were on the tree Knight was leaning against.

"I shall get my basket from my house, I will only be gone for five minutes. You can have some food with me. I have all sorts of berries in my house." Violet happily explained.

"Okay, I will have some berries with you", Leila said while smiling.

She waited for Violet next to Knight.

"We will hopefully find the platinum fountain soon", Knight said softly.

He was reassuring Leila that everything would be fine, and that they would get results quickly.

Violet was only gone for five minutes as she had stated.

"I'm back, here's the food", Violet joyfully said.

She opened the basket, there were strawberries and all sorts of unique berries with all colours of the rainbow. There were also apples, which were purple in colour. Violet also had a red bag, that crossed over her shoulder, that had a few types of juice; mixed berry juice, strawberry juice, pineapple juice and apple juice.

"You can choose whichever drink and food you would like", Violet said to both Leila and Knight.

She lay the bag gently in front of the both of them.

"I would like some purple apples with mixed berry juice, please", Knight said.

"I would like some strawberries with strawberry juice, please", Leila quietly said.

"I will have some orange berries with pineapple juice", Violet happily stated.

The three of them got their snacks and drinks. They then started eating and drinking. Whilst they were enjoying their beverages, they were all thinking where, if the platinum fountain wasn't near the outskirts of the city of ruby, then where it may be. The platinum fountain could be literally anywhere. However, the three of them knew that there would be a pattern of some sort as to where it would relocate, once a person had touched it.

Fifteen minutes later, they had all finished their beverages.

"You know what, I'm just going to use my intuition with where the platinum fountain may be located", Violet said assertively.

"Okay, so where do you feel it might be?", Knight asked.

"I feel it may be underneath the main part of the city of ruby, like in the centre, but underground, not on the surface, you know." Violet explained briefly.

"That sounds like a good idea to me", Knight said with agreement to what Violet had stated.
Knight yawned suddenly, "I feel quite tired, is it alright if I lean against this tree for ten more minutes?", Knight asked Violet.

"Yes, that's alright with me", Violet said softly.

"So, where are you from Knight?", Violet enquired to Knight.

"I'm from a city, which is quite far from here, but I like the city of ruby more, because the people seem nicer here than the city I'm from." Knight explained briefly.

"Oh, I see, so would you like to one day, once you have returned to normal, like to live here permanently in the city of ruby?" Violet asked in a curious manner.

"Maybe, I would have to think about it quite thoroughly", Knight graciously said.

"Okay", Violet said with a faint hint of happiness in her voice.

"What about you Leila, where are you from?", Violet asked.

"I am from a village where they grow lots of strawberries", Leila answered.

"I see, that explains why you like strawberries so much", Violet said and gave Leila a very gentle smile.

The outskirts of the city of ruby were very quiet. People who lived in the main city area, would go to the outskirts of the city if they wanted to be in a relaxing and quiet environment. It was also helpful, if a person just wanted to sit somewhere and think. Beautiful trees filled the landscape of the outskirts of the city, with over ten unique varieties of trees.

"I just remembered, we do have a bit of a time limit. Leila was shrunk with this unique gemstone, but it lasts for only four hours. We probably have roughly three hours or less left until she will return to her normal size." Knight briefly explained.

"I understand, in that case, if it's okay with you, because I know that you are a bit tired. We should probably go to the centre of the city of ruby now, so that we can find the platinum fountain as soon as possible", Violet eloquently pointed out.

"Do you think it's possible to find the fountain in roughly three hours or less", Leila asked Violet in a surprised tone.

"I do feel it is possible to find it in that time period, yes", Violet joyfully replied.

"I will leave my stuff here; like my bag and my basket. I will collect it once we have finished checking the centre of the city, and hopefully finding the fountain", Violet said.

They all began to walk a bit fast, but not too much so that they were straining themselves. There lay a water fountain roughly twenty metres away from where they were walking, in front of them.

"Maybe, just maybe, the platinum fountain is underneath that water fountain over there", Knight jokingly said.

"This is no time for jokes", Leila said in a frustrated tone.

"You know, he may actually be right!", Violet said in a serious manner.

The three of them started running towards the water fountain that was in sight.

"Okay, so now what do we do?", Knight asked Violet.

"I don't mean to sound rude, but since you are a rabbit, you could be the one who digs the quickest", Violet said.

"I will get to it right away!", Knight said in an excited tone.

Knight then began to dig rapidly near the base of the fountain with his two front paws. There was dirt that was being tossed all over the nearby area of where he was digging. After seven minutes of Knight continuously digging, Knight shouted;

"There is something underneath the fountain, it appears to be metallic in colour, but I can't make out exactly what it is."

The reason Knight could not make out what was exactly down there, was due to the fact that there was a bit of glitter around the object he was looking at.

"Really?", Violet enquired with amazement.

Violet, Leila and Knight began looking at the object in question. Violet was thinking to herself that the metallic object was most likely the platinum fountain. She was ninety percent certain of it.

"Okay, let's all go in!", Violet said with assertiveness in her voice.

They all carefully climbed down on sloped rocks, which seemed to be quite old. Violet moved the glitter with her hands quite forcefully, because naturally, she was eager to see what the glitter was hiding. The object preserved by the glitter was the platinum fountain. All three of them gasped and were shocked that they had found it in such a relatively small amount of time.

"I'm so happy we found it!", Knight joyfully said.
"I can't really believe it was actually where you said it was, even if you were joking, Knight", Leila said in a surprised tone.

"Well done, Knight, now all we have to do is notify the queen that the fountain is located here and accompany her and then you and Leila can go to the town in the clouds." Violet said with such happiness in her voice.

The three of them climbed out of where the platinum fountain was and began making their way to the queen's palace. Leila was still pondering as to how quick they had located the elusive fountain, it seemed to her as almost unreal and almost impossible.

"I would like to give both of you a present before you leave to the town in the clouds", Violet said in a slightly sad tone.

Violet was a bit sad, because she had grown quite fond of Leila and Knight, but they would quite soon leave the city of ruby. She was of course happy for them, but she felt sadness at the same time. She saw both Leila and Knight as very unique individuals, not because of their appearance, which was the most obvious sign that they were unique from other people. It was their lovely personalities and how they behaved that stood out to her.

"If you ever come to the city of ruby again, you can visit me", Violet added.

"Yes, I will do so", Knight stated with a soft smile on his face.

"Yes, I probably will visit again", Leila said gently.

They were walking slower than they were before, probably due to the fact Violet was upset, and Leila and Knight did not wish to walk fast, as they felt it would probably be inconsiderate. Twenty minutes later, they arrived at the queen's palace. The royal guard, who did not let them pass before was informed by Claire that they were permitted to enter the palace, once they had found the platinum fountain.

"Did you find what the queen wanted you to find?", the royal guard firmly enquired.

"Yes, we have", Violet graciously replied.

"You haven't been gone for very long, are you sure you have found exactly what the queen asked for?", the royal guard asked.

"Yes, we thankfully found it quickly, if you don't believe me, fetch the queen so that I may speak with her", Violet said in an annoyed tone.

"It's okay, I believe you, all of you three are free to pass", the royal guard reluctantly said.

Claire was walking and saw Violet, Leila and Knight come into the palace.

"You're back awfully quick!", Claire said in a surprised tone.

"We have found the platinum fountain", Violet said in a slow manner.

"Where exactly is it?", Claire curiously asked.

"Right next to the outskirts of the city, we all saw it together", Violet replied.

"Follow me", Claire told the three of them.

When they arrived outside of the queen's chamber, Claire went in to notify the queen that the fountain had been located. The queen then came out of her chamber and gasped. She genuinely couldn't believe the fountain had been found so fast.

"Where is the platinum fountain?", the queen asked.

"On the outskirts of this city", Violet answered.

Claire had told the queen where it was located from what Violet said when she just recently entered the palace, but the queen just liked to be thorough and certain of the facts.

"We can show you where it is", Knight suggested.
"Of course, like I said before, I wish to see the platinum fountain with my very own eyes", the queen said with assertion.

Leila thinking to herself and wondering why the royal guards wore pink coloured armour.

"Just out of curiosity, why do your royal guards wear armour that is pink?", Leila asked the queen.

"What do you feel when you look at the colour pink?", the queen asked Leila.

"Hmm... let me see, I feel quite happy and at ease", Leila answered.

"Exactly, so you I assume now know the reason as to why their armour is coloured pink", the queen explained with a small smile on her face.

The queen normally did not smile much, because she missed her brother, but the platinum fountain was found, and she was one hundred percent certain she would solve her brother's puzzle and find out where he left to.

"I would like to thank all three of you, for finding the elusive fountain", the queen elegantly stated.

"Actually, it was Knight who found it", Violet said.

"Interesting, regardless I know that all three of you did help with it, I am grateful to all of you", the queen said with a hint of happiness in her voice.

Chapter 9

The queen started to get ready and was being accompanied with Claire, Violet, Leila and Knight. She felt a tiny bit nervous, she had never seen her brother's ornament he made, as a result she knew it would make her feel a bit upset. She thought that hopefully soon she would see him in person. The thought of her seeing her brother again after such a long period of time brought many mixed emotions in her, naturally the predominant one was happiness.

"Let's go", the queen stated.

All five of them left the palace, and walked towards where the fountain was, with Violet leading the way. Ten minutes later, they had arrived at where the water fountain was.

"It's underneath here", Violet gently stated.

"I see", the queen said quietly.

Violet led all of them down carefully underneath and made sure that they stepped only on sturdy rocks so they would not slip.

Glitter masked the platinum fountain just like before, when Violet, Leila and Knight were there.

"Allow me, I will remove the glitter away from the fountain", Violet softly said.

The glitter was removed, and the platinum fountain was revealed.

"Oh my! This is spectacular!", the queen said in such a fascinated manner.

The queen started to study the platinum fountain, while slowly walking around it.

The queen sighed and said in a sad manner, "The reason I wanted you three to find the platinum fountain was because my brother, who disappeared made the fountain. He said on a note that I should solve the riddle of the fountain if I wish to know why he left the city of ruby, and hopefully maybe I could find where he left to."

"Well, that explains your passion and enthusiasm when we told you that we had found it. Maybe, we can all help you to try and solve the riddle of the platinum fountain your brother made." Leila eloquently suggested.

"Yes, okay", the queen quietly said.
"Maybe it has something to do with what happened to me and Leila, with regards to us turning into animals", Knight graciously suggested.

"Were your lives before you were turned into animals stressful or unpleasant?", Claire enquired to Leila and Knight.

"It was both", Leila and Knight said at the same time.

"The platinum fountain's primary function or purpose may be to enable a person's life that is stressful or unpleasant, a type of holiday or break from their ordinary life", Claire explained.

Everyone there started to ponder and think about what Claire had just suggested, and began testing her theory in thought, kind of hypothetically. A few minutes had passed, and the queen said:

"I believe that is the answer to the riddle, but it still doesn't entirely explain where my brother is, or why he left."

"It actually does because your brother most likely left the city of ruby, because it was a bit too busy and hectic for him. As a result, he left this city, and most likely went to the most quietest place in this region of the west", Claire explained with precision.

"Fascinating! You solved it so quickly, Claire. That must be the answer to the riddle. Well done", the queen acknowledged with an overwhelming amount of happiness in her voice.

"That means we are able to go to the town in the clouds, right?", Knight asked the queen.

"Yes, I will just discuss something with Claire, and I will allow you and Leila to go to the town in the clouds", the queen articulated to Knight.

Claire was wondering what the queen wanted to discuss with her. The queen wanted her to look for her brother, and wondered if Claire knew the quietest place in the region of the west. The red-haired queen began speaking to Claire. The elegant queen wished for Claire to get ready immediately and to leave as soon as possible. Minister Claire did not know where the quietest place in the region of the west was, however, she did have a vague idea of where the more peaceful and placid regions were. She was the type of person who was almost always busy, but that was the way she liked it.

A few minutes had passed, and the queen had finished discussing with Claire the arrangements for her to find her brother.

"We will all go to the palace, I will let you two enter the town in the clouds once we are in the palace, don't worry", the queen said with an excited tone in her voice.

The queen was quite overwhelmed by the fact she had a lead on her brother's whereabouts, and that she may be able to see him soon. They all headed back to the palace, once they were there, the queen got a yellow-coloured gemstone from her room. She placed the gemstone inside a mould of the exact shape of the gem, which was a typical cushion cut and was highly polished. The shade of yellow was exquisitely vibrant and rich, to the point if a person looked directly at it for more than five seconds, their eyes would sting quite a bit.

"That gem looks quite nice!", Knight suddenly blurted out.

"Yes, it was a gift from my brother years ago, it's very special to me", the queen explained.

A wooden door, that was in the room then began to open slowly.

"I know you two may think this is a joke, but it's not. There are stairs here, which lead up to a big cloud. The town is visible from there, it is only a four minute walk from the big cloud you will arrive on", the queen thoroughly explained.

"How long do we have to walk up the stairs?", Knight enquired.

"Roughly six minutes non-stop unfortunately, that is the only way there. Once you reach the big cloud, you can rest there for a bit if you would like", the queen replied.

"If you ever visit the city of ruby again, you know where my stall is. I would like to give both of you something", Violet gently said.

Violet reminded Leila and Knight that they were welcome and could visit her, once they had finished on their quest. She got out two necklaces out of one of her pockets. When Violet had gotten the beverages from her place, she had gotten both of them gifts. She suspected that the platinum fountain may have been located quite quickly, and as a result wanted to give them both something to remember her by. One of the necklaces was a circle with a vivid turquoise coloured apatite in the shape of a circle in it. The chain was thin, but not paper thin, the necklace was made out of silver. The second necklace was made from rose gold, with a square cut solitaire pink diamond. The chain was a tiny bit thicker than the other necklace.

"They're so beautiful!", Leila said in surprise.

Leila was referring to both necklaces and saw them as genuine works of art and craftsmanship. She also felt so touched that someone would wish to give her a gift so beautiful sincerely.

"I must say, those are beautiful unique pieces, with such pretty gemstones", Knight said while smiling.

"This one is for you Leila, and this one is for you Knight", Violet quietly said.

She handed Leila the rose gold necklace and the silver one to Knight. They both looked at their presents while smiling. Knight helped Leila put her necklace on. Leila done the same to Knight.
"Thank you, Violet. That is so kind and thoughtful of you!", Leila and Knight said at the same time.

"You're both very welcome!", Violet said while smiling ever so gently.

"Don't worry, once we have returned to normal, we will come back to visit you", Leila and Knight said at the same time.

"Okay, that makes me feel better, I love both of you and I hope you find what you're looking for", Violet said with both happiness and sadness in her voice.

Knight and Leila began making their way to the staircase.

"I will close the door once you both have entered", the queen stated.

"Okay", Knight said.

Both Leila and Knight started walking up the staircase and began walking fairly fast as they were curious to see what the big cloud was like. Leila would be able to wear the necklace Violet gave to her when she would shrink; like as she was at present and as a woman when she had turned back into as a person. Claire began to leave the palace and planned to hopefully have a result in a suitable duration of time. The queen was feeling tired, and made her way to her chamber to rest, looking and locating the platinum fountain had taken a lot of energy from her, as she was feeling many mixed emotions in a short span of time. Sadness was still the overwhelming emotion the queen was feeling, because she had wished still that her brother could have at least spoken to her about what was bothering him, instead of just leaving without consulting her.

Meanwhile, Jessica was squatting outside of the amethyst tower. She was waiting there for some time without moving, she was wondering if her daughter Hilda would be quite annoyed at her. Jessica felt guilty of being absent from her daughter for seventy whole years. The more she remembered the number seventy in her head, the more she realised how long it had actually been and how lonely her daughter must have felt. She decided to enter the amethyst tower via secret passage, that only her and Hilda were aware of; it was on the east side, fifty percent exactly halfway on the bottom of it there lay a keyhole. Jessica inserted a key which she had in one of her pocket like compartments in her armour. Hilda also had the same key; it was two circles intertwined. Not just anyone could use it though, both Jessica and Hilda were taught how to use it. The key was sharp everywhere, it could cut through most materials, and there was such a particular way to move it in three different phases, which had to be timed in separate timed intervals.

She turned the key in the specific ways it had to be turned in, the door, which was three feet tall only opened. Jessica walked through and saw Hilda in the distance in the tower.

"Hilda, I'm home", Jessica said

Hilda turned around and faced her mother and couldn't almost believe that her mother had actually returned.

"I can't believe you finally came back, welcome home, mum", Hilda said in an extremely surprised tone.

"I have a present for you", Jessica said with a smile on her face.

Jessica got the pink gemstone out of one of her pocket like compartments in her suit of armour; just like the key she had gotten out earlier.

"That's really pretty, that was the gemstone I saw in the book many years ago. That's so thoughtful of you, thank you", Hilda said.

"That's the reason I was away for all these years", Jessica explained.

"That's sweet, I understand, I just really missed you. That's why I asked a rabbit named Knight and a dragon named Leila to try and find you to pass the message on that I wanted you to come back", Hilda said.

Hilda assumed that Knight and Leila had successfully passed on the message to Jessica, hence her swift return from when she had asked both of them.

"Yes, I did run into them, they passed the message on to me. Knight was the one who told me about where the beautiful pink gem was located", Jessica said.

"Oh really? That's good news, they're both quite unique and useful", Hilda said in a cheerful manner.

"Well, luckily now that I am here, we can spend time together and relax a bit", Jessica gently said.

"Yes, that's true, I'm glad", Hilda said.

Leila and Knight were still walking up the stairs.

"How much longer until we reach the top?", Knight asked Leila while panting.

"I think we have walked up for about four minutes, which means we only have two minutes left", Leila replied.

"I'm almost completely out of breath, oh well I will just continue until we reach the big cloud. Like the queen said, we can just rest once we reach the big cloud", Knight said exhaustingly.

"Don't worry, you will be fine", Leila said softly.
Two minutes of them both walking up the stairs, and they had reached the big cloud. It looked more like an egg; it didn't have the usual shape of a typical cloud. That cloud was almost completely round and symmetrical but not entirely, it had a sharp curve on the upper side of it.

"That doesn't really look like a cloud to me!", Knight said with a surprised tone in his voice.

"Hmmm, you're right, but this must be the big cloud the queen was talking about", Leila said in a puzzled manner.

Both Leila and Knight were contemplating that it may be a possibility there was some sort of honest mistake the queen had made.

"Oh, the town is over there!", Knight said suddenly.

"Yes, that must be the town, this must be the correct cloud then. At least we know for certain that no mistake was made. I was getting a bit worried for a second there", Leila articulated.

"Yeah, me too I was getting a bit worried, but everything checks out fine", Knight said in a relieved tone.

When Knight and Leila had finished walking up the stairs they had landed on top of the egg-like cloud.

"Ah, I'm going to rest a little bit, if that's alright", Knight blurted out.

"Of course, you may rest, I will do the same", Leila said.

Chapter 10

Faint light pink-coloured glitter was everywhere, it was a similar shade to the pink diamond necklace that was given to Leila. Both Knight and Leila were quite fatigued and had dealt with a lot in a short span of time, hence they had not noticed the pink glitter that was part of the environment of the clouds. They had both fallen asleep, what they both did not realise was that since they were both animals, it drained a lot of their energy, which is why they would become quite tired fairly quickly. Especially Knight, because he had been an animal for four times longer than Leila and the more anyone who touches the platinum fountain is an animal for, the more energy will be drained.

The sky was a gentle peach colour, flower petals of all colours were floating all around the atmosphere. A woman wearing a long turquoise metallic robe approached Leila and Knight.

"Excuse me, are you two alright?", the lady enquired.

Both Knight and Leila woke up instantly upon the lady asking her question.

"Yeah, we're okay, just a bit tired unfortunately", Knight replied swiftly.

He was a bit annoyed that his nap had been disturbed.

"I come from that town over there, I occasionally patrol the surrounding area", the lady said.

"We were actually just heading there now, me and my friend Leila just wanted to rest here a bit. While we are on the subject of that town, do you know anyone there who knows anything about the platinum fountain?", Knight asked curiously.

"Well, yes, but don't tell anyone in the town I told you this; whenever someone touches the platinum fountain they only turn into an animal if their life at the time of when they touched the fountain is difficult and very hectic in a negative way meaning. You will only return as people once you have fully recuperated from how your life was. The mistake you and your friend Leila are making is that you are seeing the fact you are animals as a derogatory thing, but I know it sounds weird, although you should actually enjoy it. Otherwise, you won't turn return as you were before, I would know because it happened to me." The lady explained in detail.

"That sounds quite strange", Leila said.

"It does, in a way, but not really when you think about it", the lady said.

"What's your name?", Knight enquired.

"My name is Linda, and yours, meaning both of you?", Linda asked in a placid manner.
"My name is Leila and his is Knight", Leila answered.

"You both have very unique nice names", Linda stated.

"So, what you are basically saying is I'm supposed to enjoy being a red rabbit?", Knight asked in an annoyed manner.

Knight was contemplating if there was another way in him and Leila returning to normal than just enjoying it and waiting it out.

"Yes, because that is the only way of you and your friend Leila returning to normal that I know of. The reason you turned into animals in the first place is due to the fact you needed a break as I said before", Linda reiterated.

"I shouldn't really say this, but that sucks", Leila said in an irritated manner.

"Then again, the brother of the queen of the city of ruby is the one who made it. You could try and find him and ask him if there is another way of you both returning as people other than what I have already mentioned", Linda said calmly.

"I'm on board with that idea, what about you Leila?", Knight asked Leila.

"Yes, we might as well, but is it alright if we rest in that town over there?", Knight asked Linda.

"That's fine with me, however we need to make sure that no one sees both of you", Linda said.

"Why's that?", Knight enquired in a very puzzled manner.

To Knight it didn't seem to make sense that people living in a town would have an issue with two animals walking in there.

"The people living in the town do not like the platinum fountain, I do not know why, but it's better not to mention it at all to them. Since you and your friend are both animals and you can talk that would attract attention from the people in the town and would cause the platinum fountain having to be mentioned. It's basically just better if I hide both of you and take you to my house and you can rest there", Linda explained thoroughly.

"Okay, that sounds good to me", Knight stated.

"Yeah, I'm alright with that", Leila said.

"The problem is that I just remembered quite soon you will return to your regular size Leila. Probably what's best is if you return to your normal size and then you just shrink immediately after that, therefore you will have more time that way", Knight pointed out.
"That's true Knight, I will do that", Leila said swiftly.

Leila returned to her normal size.

"You're quite big, but I guess that's normal for a dragon", Linda stated.

Knight handed Leila the green-coloured gemstone. She shrunk herself and handed back the gem to Knight.

"Okay so now we have four additional hours, right?", Leila asked Knight.

Leila just wanted Knight to check if she remembered the number of hours to be exactly correct.

"Yes, that is correct", Knight answered with enthusiasm in his voice.

Knight was strongly against enjoying life as a rabbit, hence he had become enthusiastic by the fact there may have been another way of returning to normal besides that.

"Did you get that gemstone from Jessica?", Linda enquired curiously.

"Yes, we did, do you know Jessica?", Leila asked.

"I do, I was the one who taught Jessica many things", Linda said.

"That's interesting, do you have any interesting gemstones; like some that may return me and my friend to normal?", Knight asked Linda with excitement.

"Unfortunately, I do not, I have some colourful pretty gems. However, I do not have any practically useful gems, sorry Knight", Linda said.

"That's a shame", Knight said in a disappointed tone.

"I have a bag with me here, both of you will probably have to get in here so you're not seen", Linda stated bluntly.

The bag which Linda had was a metallic silver colour and was fairly big, it was rectangular. Leila and Knight hopped in the bag.

"Okay, I will go straight to my house from here, don't leave the bag until I tell you it's okay to do so", Linda explained.

Leila and Knight acknowledged what Linda had said by nodding. She then closed the bag, and she started walking on a path that led from the big cloud to the town. The path was a glossy bright red colour, it was extremely smooth, and immaculately clean. There were guard rails, which were a rich gold colour to prevent anyone walking from falling. Had the path been sloped a person could slide down it, due to how smooth it was. Linda was walking fast, because she wanted to have one of her mixed berry smoothies which she would make often. Two minutes later, she had arrived at her house. The house was dark green in colour and was made entirely of solid marble. It was completely carved out of marble, all of the houses in the town were constructed of marble. She walked through the door and entered into the living room. It was very spacious because Linda had a gymnasium as part of the room as she enjoyed practising gymnastics, it was one of her hobbies. There was also weightlifting equipment there.

"You can both come out now", Linda said gently.

"Are you sure?", Knight enquired.

"Yes, I am sure I am in my house now", Linda replied.

Leila and Knight both hopped out of the bag. They both began looking around and were surprised at how fancy the interior of Linda's house was.

"Your house is really elegant, did you decorate it yourself?", Leila asked Linda.

"Of course, all of us in the town in the clouds make our own houses and decorate them ourselves", Linda explained with a smile on her face.

"I would like to have a similar kind of house like this one day", Knight mentioned while studying the ceiling of the house.

The ceiling of the house had multi-coloured marble that had been cut into pieces which formed a large picture. Different types of ribbons were what the marble displayed. Linda was fond of different ribbons and would collect them and even make her own.

"Mind, it does take quite long to build you know", Linda explained.

"How long, roughly?", Knight asked Linda curiously.

"My house took twenty-five years, while others in this town have worked on their houses for fifty years even, but that's only if the house is quite large", Linda stated.

Linda showed Knight and Leila where they could sit. It was a velvet turquoise sofa.

"Would you both like some mixed berry smoothies?", Linda enquired.

"Yes, please", Leila and Knight both replied.

"Okay, I will make it now", Linda said.
She opened a door and entered the kitchen; it was on the left side of the living room. She had a basket of mixed berries on the table and took a handful of them in both her hands. She then placed them in a pestle and mortar that was made out of solid pinewood. Linda was once a jeweller in the town in the clouds but decided to just pursue a simpler lifestyle. She began grinding the assortment of berries, after that she mixed them with some water. Once she had mixed the water and berries entirely in a jug, she poured the smoothie into three triangular shaped glasses.

"Here you are", Linda said gently.

She handed Leila and Knight their smoothies from a brass-coloured tray, which held the three glasses.

"Thank you, Linda,", Leila and Knight said simultaneously.

"It's nice to relax you know", Linda stated while reclining on a fuchsia-coloured armchair.

Leila and Knight were sipping their berry smoothies in a placid manner as they wished to enjoy every bit of their drinks.

"Yes, it is", Leila mentioned in response to Linda's statement.

"You know I used to be a jeweller here in the town in the clouds, but the people here were quite amazed and pleased with my work. The problem was that when I first started it, I done it because I enjoyed doing it, however after people started liking my work a lot, I started to see my work more as a job than an enjoyable hobby that I had." Linda explained thoroughly.

"Oh, I understand, I assume that was when you touched the platinum fountain, isn't it?", Leila asked while looking at Linda's eyes.

"That is correct, you're good at piecing events together, aren't you?", Linda rhetorically asked.

"To be honest it's fairly obvious, considering what you said to me and Knight so far", Leila stated.

"You're as perceptive as ever", Linda stated while glaring at Leila.

"What do you mean by that?", Leila enquired in a puzzled manner.

"I hope this doesn't upset you, but your mother asked me to keep an eye on you when you were in the village of strawberries, so I would check on you occasionally to make sure you were safe and not struggling", Linda explained in a firm way.

Leila was digesting what Linda had said and felt relieved that she had been looked after even though at the time she was not aware of it.

"Well, that's nice to know", Leila said with a sigh of relief.
"Your mother will see you once you have sorted out certain things, she just wanted you to learn things by yourself", Linda articulated.

"That sounds interesting!", Knight suddenly said with a medium sized smile on his face.

"I must make you aware though before I say anything with regards to the queen's brother, that looking for him may take longer than just waiting it out and enjoying the way you are now", Linda said firmly.

"In other words, you do not advise me or Knight to look for the queen's brother, right?", Leila stated.

"Correct, you would be making a mistake and you would only realise it when you are about halfway of reaching him, he's always on the move, you know", Linda bluntly said.

"I thought he just went to a quiet place where he could relax", Leila said with a surprised tone.

"That's what he wants you to think, it isn't easy to find him", Linda said in an annoyed tone.

"How do you know so much about him?", Leila enquired while studying Linda.

"We used to be close friends, but he cut off with me because he wanted to be completely alone", Linda said.

"I see, so Knight what do you think?", Leila asked him gently.

"What do you mean?", Knight asked in a confused manner.

"Do you want to just wait it out and enjoy life as a rabbit, or do you want to find the queen's brother?", Leila asked Knight in a slightly annoyed tone.

"I don't know, I need a bit of time to think about it", Knight reluctantly stated.

Linda was annoyed at the fact Knight was reluctant in waiting it out, because she knew much more than him. The solution could be simple and easy in theory. Leila was also a little bit annoyed at Knight.

"Alright, we can wait it out, if that makes you happy Linda since me and Leila don't really have a choice", Knight reluctantly said.

"You do have a choice Knight, however you must understand that it would just take excessively longer, which doesn't make sense if you want to turn back to normal in the quickest way possible", Linda explained while glaring at Knight.

"So, is there a funfair or something nearby where I can try and enjoy myself?", Knight enquired sarcastically.

"There is one, but not in the town in the clouds, it is located in a place known as silver village", Linda answered attentively.

Linda was aware that Knight was being sarcastic, but it would do him some good if he did go to the funfair she recommended, he would relax and may enjoy himself she thought to herself.

"Are you up for that Leila?", Knight softly enquired.

"Do they have the teacup ride, Linda?", Leila asked inquisitively.

"Yes, they do it's quite nice, they do require a payment of three silver coins per person per day at the funfair mind", Linda pointed out.

"What a coincidence, I happen to have six silver coins on me at the moment, I've had them for quite a while because I didn't really need to use it", Knight said with a smile on his face.

"I'm up for that!", Leila said in a loud manner.

Leila was happy, hence the loud manner in which she affirmed her interest in the funfair. Linda knew that if Knight and Leila pulled this off correctly, they could return to normal much quicker than they thought.

"I have a request though Linda", Leila stated firmly.

"Yes, what's that?", Linda asked in a surprised tone.

"Could you come with me and Knight, it would be more fun that way, what do you think?", Leila asked.

Linda began thinking about her schedule, which wasn't busy, however she wanted to come up with an excuse, because she was concerned Knight would annoy her while they're all at the funfair.

"Well, I have to meet a friend soon, so I'm not really sure if I could go you know", Linda said in a hesitant manner.

"That's a shame, I thought you could help me and Knight", Leila said in a sad tone.

"Since it is that important to you, I will come along. Don't worry, I have my own three silver coins", Linda stated while sighing.

Linda knew of other funfairs, which were located around the perimeter of the town in the clouds, however those funfairs were quite hectic and noisy. She wanted both Leila and Knight to attend the quieter funfair, so they could try and enjoy themselves. Another good thing about the one she recommended to both of them was that it had more rides and a better variety of them.

"Silver village is located four miles from the town in the clouds, once you're on ground level that is", Linda said in a slightly slow manner.

Leila was fond of the teacup ride, because she used to go on it in the village of strawberries when she was a little girl.

The one she rode on was faster than usual. The thought of her going on a teacup ride with Knight and Linda made her quite happy, due to the fact before she was always alone when she would ride on it.

As for Knight, this would be his first time attending a funfair, he would hear about them where he was from, but he never actually went to one nor went on any rides. He had heard from people that the food at the funfairs was quite unique and tasty, which is what he was thinking about. He was scared of going on the rides, because he didn't know what to expect. The way most funfairs worked was that you pay an admission fee and all the food you would like is free. Knight was hoping the arrangement of the one he was going to attend was like that, otherwise he may not be able to try any of the food; he only had enough for Leila's and his admission fee.

"So, shall we go?", Linda asked both Knight and Leila.

"Yes, let's go", Leila replied enthusiastically.

"Yeah, let's go to the funfair", Knight said with a hint of a sarcastic tone in his voice.

"Oh yeah, I forgot, is it okay if I use this gemstone on you Leila? It will keep you permanently the size you are now until you return to how you used to be as a person", Linda asked gently.

The gem was a bright orange colour, it spiralled upwards; it looked more like an ornament than a gemstone, however this was a rough gem it had not been cut ever.

"Yes, okay that would solve my problem of always worrying about the time limit of the gem that shrinks me", Leila said happily.

"Well, that makes my life easier, I do not have to excessively worry about losing the gemstone. I don't want to lose it, but you know I know that if I lose it, then poor Leila cannot go to certain places because people may get scared if they see a dragon as big as Leila", Knight explained in a relieved tone.

"That's not very nice, you know Knight, Leila is the love of your life", Linda stated bluntly.

Leila and Knight froze in shock. They were both surprised that Linda knew that both of them loved each other a lot. The two of them stared at each other without blinking. That lasted for one minute.

"That's a bit of a bold statement, Linda, you don't know that for certain", Knight said in a fast manner.

"Oh, but I do, you two should get married once you have returned to normal, what do you think?", Linda enquired to both of them.

Leila had gotten to terms with what Linda had said and thought that it would have come up sooner or later that she loved Knight. As for him, he wasn't taking it as well, because he planned on telling Leila that he loved her only when they had both returned to normal as people.

"We might as well do that", Knight said reluctantly.

"Yes, that would be nice", Leila happily said while smiling at Knight.

"Most likely within one day of spending time at the funfair you will both return as people, just to clarify", Linda stated while smiling at both of them.

"Why didn't you mention this before?", Knight enquired.

"Because you never asked, but anyway I'm going to get my glider out so we can go to the funfair now, don't worry all of us will be able to ride on it", Linda said.

Chapter 11

The glider Linda got out was glossy bright pink in colour, this was so that it was clearly visible when she was flying in the sky. The glider was hexagonal in shape and the fabric was quite thick for a glider to add stability, otherwise it would change direction in a sudden way.

"Okay, get on both of you", Linda softly said.

Both Leila and Knight reluctantly got on, they were both a bit uneasy with heights.

"Don't worry, it will only take two minutes to get to the funfair", Linda said to comfort them.

She took the glider outside on a balcony and put both her hands on the glider and threw herself off. The wind was strong, it took them two hundred metres away from her house in a split second. Luckily, Linda knew exactly what she was doing, she was extremely skilled in using the glider. She went in the direction of where the ground was. The funfair was located on ground level, but on the outskirts of the town in the clouds. Two minutes had passed.

"We are here, see it wasn't that scary", Linda stated while smiling.

Both of Knight's and Leila's eyes were closed firmly. Leila was uneasy around heights but when she was flying as a dragon she wasn't, this was because she was the one in control of how she was flying and she didn't fly too far above the ground. Leila saw it as a bit different. They both opened their eyes realising they weren't flying anymore.

"It was a bit", Knight said in a lethargic way.

"Only a tiny bit", Leila said in an excited manner.

Knight wasn't concerned of heights when he would fly on Leila's back, because he knew that she wouldn't do anything too reckless and she wouldn't fly too far above the ground anyway.

The funfair was quite large; it was as big as a town. It was completely domed with a mint green velvet cloth. There were eight entrances around the whole domed venue. There was a man standing outside the entrance where Linda, Knight and Leila were. He was wearing a polar bear costume. It was quite well made, it appeared as though he was a real polar bear standing on two feet.

"Hey, that is a nice suit, I like it", Knight suddenly said upon seeing the polar bear costume.

"Thank you, little rabbit", the man answered back while gently smiling at Knight.
"Leila, Knight this is my husband Daniel, he works at this funfair, he likes it because he can have fun here", Linda said in a placid manner.

"I see, well I could understand why he would want to work here, it seems fun, lively and relaxing", Leila said happily.

"It is, and I hope you and your rabbit friend relax, have fun and enjoy yourselves here. Seeing people happy here is also one of the reasons I like this job", Daniel mentioned.

"Daniel, could you advise me on what is the best and most fun ride here?", Knight enquired with curiosity.

Daniel began thinking for a minute.

"Well, there are at least four extremely fun rides. All the rides in this funfair are obviously enjoyable and exciting, however the ones that stick out the most are; ride number thirteen, twenty, thirty four and forty one. The rides are all numbered and those are the ones in my opinion that are most fun", Daniel explained tranquilly.

"Okay, could you write the numbers down for me, because that's an assortment of random numbers that I wouldn't remember?", Knight requested.

"Actually, Linda would you remember the ride numbers that I mentioned just now?", Daniel asked Linda in a gentle way.

"Yes, I would", Linda affirmed with certainty.

"Perfect, then I will just rely on you to remember them and Knight can go on his fun rides", Daniel stated in a joyful way.

"Don't worry Knight, I will go with you on those rides in case you get scared", Leila said in a gentle way.

"Thank you, Leila", Knight stated with a hint of sarcasm in his voice.

"Knight, there is something I think you would find interesting, it's near ride number thirteen. It's around sixteen metres away from the ride", Daniel suggested.

"What is there?", Knight enquired inquisitively.

"It's better if you just see it for yourself", Daniel replied while gently smiling at Knight.

"Leila, there is someone I would like you to see", Linda stated.

"Does that mean me and Knight will be separated?", Leila asked in a concerned way.

"Yes, but not for very long, you will still be able to go on the rides together. While Knight is looking at what's near ride number thirteen, I will show you to the person", Linda explained softly.

"That should be fine then", Leila gently said.

"Don't worry sweetie, remember there is nothing to worry about", Linda said in an ever so gentle manner.

"I might as well go with you three, someone else can just take my place here", Daniel said.

"When was this funfair founded?", Leila asked.

"Around three thousand years ago", Daniel answered.

"Did you used to be a Knight, Daniel?", Knight enquired.

"Yes, well done your perceptive skills are quite good, what made you know that I was once a Knight?", Daniel replied while looking at Knight's eyes.

"I could tell by the way your demeanour is, I know how Knights are fairly well, you know", Knight articulated.

"I assume that is why you got the nickname Knight, because you also used to be one, am I correct?", Daniel stated.

"Yes, that is the case", Knight answered cheerfully.

"Well, I might as well tell you know, what I want you to see is a stall that sells interesting suits of armour, I think you may like one or two", Daniel said.

"Hmmm, that would be fascinating I do like studying and looking at different suits of armour, that would cheer me up quite a bit. I like where this is going", Knight stated in an uplifted manner.

"I will lead you to the stall, Knight", Daniel said softly.

Daniel opened the two curtain-like barriers, which sealed the entrance.

"Oh! I just remembered I need to give you six silver coins; three for me and three for Leila. Linda told me about the admission fee", Knight suddenly said.

"Don't worry about that, I think Linda just wanted to make sure you had some money on you so that you could purchase some nice souvenirs for yourself and Leila", Daniel calmly stated.

"That is exactly right Daniel, you know me well", Linda said while smiling at Daniel.

The four of them entered into the funfair. Knight and Leila gasped upon entering. They both had never seen anything so radiant and lively in their whole life.

"Yes, it is quite amazing, this funfair is not like any ordinary one. I once came here as a young man and I was quite upset, hence why I came here and upon seeing this I became happy. This place can make you happy effortlessly", Daniel happily explained.

Leila and Knight had heard everything Daniel had said and were looking around and studying the funfair in fascination. The vibrancy of the colours on the rides and around the whole place were so rich, Leila began wondering where such vivid colours were extracted from.

"Where do they extract the colours from?", Leila enquired with fascination.

"Believe it or not, they are extracted by crushing different coloured gemstones into powder and then by mixing them with water, there's a specific way to do it though, unfortunately I'm not aware of that detail", Daniel explained serenely.

"It's simple, but effective", Leila commented.

"I couldn't agree more", Daniel stated.

Leila's mother was the person that Linda wanted Leila to see. After four minutes of walking, Daniel showed Knight where the stall was that sold the different unique pieces of armour.

"This is one of the advantages of this particular funfair, you can find all sorts of unique merchandise that can only be bought from here. I know it may sound like I'm just saying that, but it is true. Anyway, I will let you decide on what you think for yourself, because I think you know quite a bit about what good armour is like", Daniel articulated enthusiastically.

"Oh! This is glass armour, I have only heard of rumours about it, but I never expected it to actually exist, let alone in a funfair!", Knight said with such surprise in his voice.

"You know about how that armour works I assume?", Daniel enquired.

"Of course, the glass is carved in a certain way so that when sunlight passes through it creates a rainbow ray of colour that temporarily blinds any person within a five-metre radius", Knight stated in a fascinated manner.

"Correct, however you probably know this as well, but it cannot be used in the nighttime naturally, moonlight is not as bright or invasive as sunlight, nevertheless it is extremely useful and rare", Daniel pointed out.

The lady at the stall was happy that Knight had taken such an interest in her stall.

"Hello, little rabbit!", the lady greeted Knight.

"Hi, I'm Knight, what's your name?", Knight asked.

"My name is Heather, nice to meet you", Heather replied.

"It's nice to meet you too", Knight said happily.

Knight began looking at each suit of armour on the stall and the suits of armour which were upright with a scrutinous gaze.

"I really like this one!", Knight abruptly stated.

"I like that one as well, the feather armour", Daniel said.

The feather armour was comprised of metal feathers, that are formed into a suit of armour, there are gaps, however it was made with practicality and efficiency in mind. It was coloured metallic dark red.
"Alright, let's get down to business, so how much for the feather armour, Heather?", Knight asked softly.

"That would be three gold coins, please", Heather replied.

"Okay, there's a bit of a problem, um, I have six silver coins, but three are for my friend Leila. That would mean I only have three silver coins", Knight said in a slightly upset tone.

"That is not a problem, here we value silver coins more than gold coins as a ratio of three to one. In other words, it would only cost you one silver coin", Heather happily stated.

"Well, that's a huge relief, I didn't want to leave this funfair empty handed after seeing that armour", Knight said in a relieved way.

"Another point is the feather armour is foldable, you know", Heather stated in a playful manner.

"I'm curious, how foldable is it?", Knight enquired with a gentle smile.

"Each piece can fold so that it's one square metre, quite portable", Heather remarked.

"Here is the silver coin", Knight said.

"Thank you very much, little rabbit", Heather softly said.

Knight handed Heather the silver coin by jumping on to where her stall was and placing the coin on the palm of her hand.

"Do you want me to give the feather armour to Daniel, so he can hang on to it, because you wouldn't be able to carry it at the moment?", Heather stated in a placid manner.

"Um, okay, that would be the most logical thing to do, after all I have some funfair rides I would like to go on anyway", Knight replied graciously.

"What I can do for you Knight is since the armour is foldable as Heather mentioned. I can put it in my locker and once you have finished your rides and hopefully you will return to normal after that, then I can give you the armour and you will be able to wear it", Daniel recommended.

"You know that is a good idea, I really like the sound of it, yeah I'm on board with that", Knight replied with enthusiasm in his voice.

Heather folded the metallic red armour and handed it to Daniel.

"Would you be able to carry all of that Daniel?", Heather enquired in a concerned way.

"I'm not too sure actually", Daniel replied.

The armour set had also come with a helmet, gauntlets, sabatons and even a shield. It weighed quite a lot, as a result

Daniel was not certain that he would be able to carry the whole set of the armour. He picked up as many as he could.

"I will carry the rest Daniel, how far is your locker?", Heather asked.

"About two minutes away from here", Daniel replied.

"So, Knight, what we will do is me and Daniel will carry the armour to his locker and then we will come straight back", Heather said while smiling at Knight.

"Okay, thanks", Knight said.

Heather and Daniel made their way to the locker. Four minutes later, they arrived back to where Knight was.

"All done", Daniel said in a happy manner.

Linda was walking with Leila fairly slowly.

"I will need you to close your eyes and I will call her over, okay Leila? Otherwise, it wouldn't be a surprise", Linda said softly.

"That's okay with me", Leila replied.

Linda walked across to where Leila's mother was and briefly spoke with her.

"You may open your eyes", Leila's mother said in an ever so gentle manner.

She opened her eyes slowly, once her eyes were open, she gasped with such surprise.

"Mother? Where did you go?", Leila asked in a soft way.

"I'm so sorry, my sweet and only daughter, I know this sounds harsh, but I left you alone because I wanted you to become completely self reliant", Leila's mother replied in a tender manner.

Leila's mother was the type of person who always spoke in an extremely gentle and soft way, it was one of her traits she was known for. Her name was Jewel, one of her other traits she was known for was her beauty as well as being extremely kind and considerate. Her hair was blush pink in colour and went all the way down to her ankles. Her eyes were turquoise which shone with such vibrancy. Her bones were quite big and was fairly tall; six foot seven to be precise. She would always wear pink coloured pearl beads around her neck which would match her hair colour. Strength was one of her other traits, both internally and externally. A lot of people saw Jewel as a role model for many reasons.

"I understand mother, I'm just so glad that you're here now", Leila happily said.

They both hugged and held each other tightly. They then began to cry; they had been apart for a long time.

"Aw, that's so sweet", Linda said.

Chapter 12

While Leila and Knight were at the funfair Claire was surveying the land of the underground of where the city of ruby was. The underground had even greener grass than on the surface. Trees were larger and most importantly Claire thought it was quiet and peaceful. It was more or less the ideal habitat that the queen's brother may have gone to. Claire had been here before, however she would always appreciate the beauty of the place. The queen's brother's name was Leo. Claire decided to just try shouting his name and hoping he may just come out if he was nearby.

"Leo! Are you there? Leo!", Claire shouted quite loudly.

There were some leaves rustling in a bush. A man jumped out quickly.

"Who are you?", Leo asked sternly.

"I am Claire, I am one of the queen's ministers in the city of ruby", Claire remarked.

"Did my sister send you?", Leo enquired.

"Ah! So you must be Leo then, it's strange the queen didn't actually fill me in with regards to what you looked like, oh well at least I found you", Claire said placidly.

"Did she solve the riddle of the platinum fountain?" Leo enquired again.

"I think so, it's to do with you leaving the city, because you wanted to rest from the hectic lifestyle you once lived, correct?", Claire stated.

"Yes, that's correct, but there is more to it than just that", Leo said in a slightly annoyed tone.

"Okay, well luckily I found you, is it okay if you visit your sister she misses you a lot you know", Claire said in a firm way.

Claire knew that Leo was fairly stubborn from briefly speaking with him just now, as a result she realised it was needed for her to be quite firm and almost strict with him, because she knew Leo also missed his sister. Claire was understanding of the fact that Leo didn't like the busy city of ruby, however she knew it was more important for him to visit his sister, because the queen was becoming significantly more upset over the past several years.

"Okay, even though my sister didn't fully solve the riddle, I will let it slide and I will go with you to visit her, mind I know the way back", Leo stated.

"I know you know the way back to the castle, however I left with the task of bringing you back, so I would prefer if I come back to the castle with you", Claire said in a happy tone of voice.

"Okay, let's go, I do miss my sister a lot. I will apologise to her upon arrival, because I do feel quite bad about the fact I haven't seen her in a long time", Leo said in a sad tone.

Claire and Leo began making their way to the ladder, which was the method of climbing back up to the city of ruby. It was located a mile from where they were currently.

They were walking for twenty minutes until they reached the ladder. After three minutes of climbing the ladder they had reached the top and came up onto a patch of grass.

"Luckily, that didn't take too long", Claire said in an enthusiastic manner.

"Yeah, that's true, thank you Claire for making me realise the importance of me visiting my sister", Leo said slowly.

"You're very welcome", Claire said while smiling at Leo.

Leo would wear robes, which were completely silver in colour. They were not very loose, but they were not tight. His hair was jet black and completely straight; it went down to his ankles. They both headed in the direction of the castle. After five minutes they had arrived at the entrance of the palace. Claire opened the door slowly. The queen was in the main room.

"I'm back and luckily, I found your brother relatively quickly my queen", Claire said in a joyous way.

The queen turned around and saw her brother standing beside Claire.

"Leo, you are finally here, welcome home!", the queen said in such a relieved and happy manner.

Before Leo replied she ran towards him and hugged him tightly. This surprised Leo, because he thought that his sister missed him, but what he assumed that it wasn't that much. He was quite wrong about that fact. He felt guilty of leaving in the first place when he realised how much his sister missed him and cared about him.

"I'm so sorry my sister, I should have never left", Leo said in a sad tone.

"I'm so happy that you're here. Leo, you do have to understand I was worried about you, if you just explained why you left, I would have felt better and if you had occasionally visited me", the queen explained in a precise manner.

"You're right, queen", Leo said in an apologetic tone.

"You know you do not have to address me that way, you're my brother. Would you like to move in with me in this castle?", the queen stated.

"Yes, because it was wrong of me to leave, I should have just explained to you what was bothering me", Leo explained.

"Well, I'm just glad that you're here now and am glad that you would like to move in with me", the queen said in a gentle manner.

The queen and her brother Leo were both relieved and joyful.

With regards to Knight and Leila, they were both making their way to meet up so they could go on their funfair rides.

After a minute and a half of both of them walking; Knight said

"Hello Leila, how are you? I know it hasn't been long, but I just wanted to check on you know"

"I feel very happy actually, more than usual, because my mother's here now", Leila replied to Knight.

Leila and Knight decided to change their plans and just go on a teacup ride instead of the rides that Daniel had recommended. After twenty minutes, which was how long the teacup ride was, they both returned to normal. Leila was how she was just before she had touched the platinum fountain and the same was with Knight.

"It seemed since they loved each other so much that after relaxing together for only twenty minutes, that was sufficient for them to return back to the way they used to be", Linda said in a surprised and happy tone of voice.

Both Leila and Knight went to a café and spoke for thirty minutes. They had decided to get married in the city of ruby and had both agreed that they would also live there. They would also visit Violet.

Milton Keynes UK
Ingram Content Group UK Ltd.
UKHW051138301124
451915UK00017B/547

9 781917 601122